Anne Forsyth

Tall Tale Tom

Illustrated by Val Biro

MACDONALD YOUNG BOOKS

Chapter One

"Well, I don't believe a word of it," said the grey cat.

"Please yourself," said Tom, the black and white cat.

The other cats sat around, their eyes like saucers in the light from the street lamp.

"What an amazing story!" said the little ginger cat. She thought Tom was wonderful.

He told such tales of his adventures. How he'd flown over the North Pole, then landed on an iceberg and made friends with the polar bears.

How he'd saved a beautiful princess and she had given him a golden collar.

"Where is it then?" said Smudge, the grey cat.

Tom loved making up stories. Ever since he was a kitten, he'd told tall stories – stories with himself as hero. You would never have known to look at him. He was black and white. He looked just like any old cat. There were dozens like him wandering about the town, hunting or scrounging in the dustbins.

But Tom was different. For one thing, he didn't have a home. Sometimes, he sat outside the back door of the butcher's shop, hoping for scraps. Sometimes he slept under the bushes in the park. Most of the time, he lay in the sun, making up stories.

Of course, everyone knew that the stories weren't true. But wasn't it great that Tom could invent such tales!

"Stories!" sniffed Smudge. "Why can't you get a proper job like everyone else? Look at Toby – he works at the fish and chip shop. Look at Tibs – she helps at the school. If you *could* get a proper job, which I doubt."

Tom was very annoyed by this. "'Course I could get a job," he said. "Give me a day or two."

He thought hard about it. He had to have a special job. Something exciting and adventurous.

Next day, Smudge met him by the harbour, sauntering along the quay.

"Hello, Tom, you got a job yet?"

"Who, me?" Tom woke up with a start. He had been making up a story about pirates and how he became a pirate cat.

"Oh yes," he said mysteriously, "I won't be around for a bit. I'm off to sea. Yo, ho, ho . . ." he added.

"A sea cat?" said Smudge.

"That's right," said Tom. He had only thought of it that very minute. "I'm going to sea."

The more he thought about it, the more he liked the idea. Fresh air, adventure, and best of all, fish on the menu every day. He waved goodbye to Smudge and trotted off as fast as his paws would take him.

The first boat he saw was the *Daisy Belle*, a fishing boat that sailed up the coast fishing for herring and cod. The captain and his mate were busy swabbing the deck and loading fish boxes.

Tom sniffed the air. "There's a funny-looking cat on the quay," said the mate, glancing up from his work. He liked animals and had a cat of his own at home.

"Don't encourage it," said the captain, who wasn't nearly as fond of cats.

But Tom paid no attention. He liked the look of the friendly mate, so he decided then and there, that he would sail on the *Daisy Belle*. So he hung around the harbour until night time.

Then he made his way back to the *Daisy Belle*. She was all ready to sail on the morning tide.

Tom jumped and landed softly on all four paws, right on the deck.

He curled up behind the fish boxes and was soon fast asleep.

When he woke, he could hear a strange sound. Chug, chug, chug. The harbour wall seemed to be moving. "No, it's the boat that's moving," he said to himself. "We're off!" The sound was the engine.

He curled up again. "How calm the sea is! This is the life for me, and no mistake."

But before long, the *Daisy Belle* sailed out of the harbour and reached the open sea. The little boat began to roll. She rose and fell, surging up and down over the huge white-crested waves.

"She's tossing a bit," said Tom to himself.

He was rather proud of knowing that boats are always called 'she', not 'it'. "I must remember that," he thought. "Because after all, I *am* a sea-going cat . . ."

Just then, the mate noticed something moving behind the stack of fish boxes. "What on earth!" he said. "Well, would you look at this!"

"It's that cat," he called to the captain. "The one we saw on the quay."

"A stowaway!" said the captain. "Well, he'll just need to stay on board till we get back."

All night long, the boat heaved up and down, and Tom with it. All night long, he lay and groaned. He felt very ill indeed. Early in the morning, the men pulled in the nets full of fish, while the gulls screeched overhead. But Tom paid no attention.

14

"I've been very stupid," he said. "I wish I'd never thought of being a sea-going cat."

At last the boat chugged her way back into harbour. The mate threw a fish to Tom, but Tom just shuddered and wouldn't touch it. He still felt very poorly.

As soon as he could, he jumped on to the quay. How good it was to feel dry land beneath his paws again!

"Hello, Tom!" It was Smudge, who just happened to be on the quay. "Are you feeling all right?" he asked.

"Me? Yes, fine!" said Tom bravely.

"So when are you going to sea again?" said Smudge, with a grin.

"Never, ever," said Tom, and hurried away as fast as he could.

Behind him, he could hear Smudge laughing.

Chapter Two

For a day or two Tom lay low. Then one morning, he felt strong enough to wander out and about. And of course, before very long, he bumped into Smudge.

"Hello," said Smudge. "Got another job yet? You *are* going to work, aren't you? Not lie around telling stories?"

"Of course," said Tom. "As a matter of fact, I've got a job," he added.

The other cats crowded round, eager to know what Tom was going to do next.

"It's at the Big House," he said without thinking. The Big House was the grandest house in the whole county. It had vast gardens and a long drive that led to the house.

"Really!" Even Smudge thought this was very splendid.

"I'm going to be chief cat there," said Tom.

"Good for you," said the other cats.

"Bet they give you a silver dish."

"Salmon *every* day – caught by the Duke himself," said the little ginger cat. "You are clever, Tom."

Tom waved his paw in a lordly way and strolled down the road to the Big House.

Round the corner, out of sight of the other cats, he stopped and thought, "What *have* I said!"

Because he hadn't got a job. Not at the Big House. Not anywhere. He was making it up. He remembered his mother, Tabitha Cat, saying, "You'll get into trouble one of these days, see if you don't. Making up stories is one thing. Telling untruths is another. You will always be Found Out."

Too late! If only he'd remembered this. And now he was sure to be in trouble, because all the cats, especially Smudge, would expect him to be Chief Cat at the Big House.

19

There was only one thing to do. He would have to get a job at the Big House.

He reached the great iron gates. Beyond them, the drive seemed to stretch for miles. He trotted along the drive until he came to the front door. Then he said to himself, "Working cats go to the back door."

He found his way to the back of the house, took a deep breath and tapped on the door with his paw.

It was opened by the cook – an angry looking woman with a red face. She looked down at Tom, and before he could say, "Have you a job for a keen, clever cat?" there was a growl.

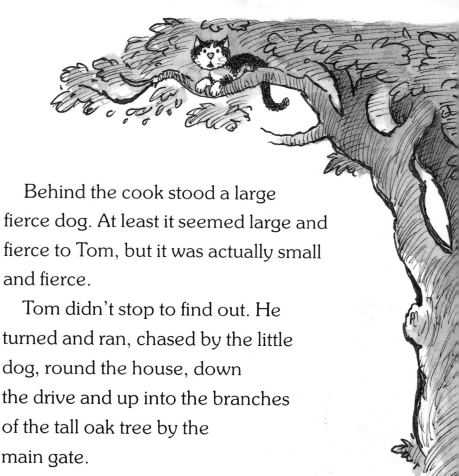

Behind the cook stood a large
fierce dog. At least it seemed large and
fierce to Tom, but it was actually small
and fierce.

Tom didn't stop to find out. He
turned and ran, chased by the little
dog, round the house, down
the drive and up into the branches
of the tall oak tree by the
main gate.

The little dog kept snapping and
jumping. Tom climbed higher and higher.

After a bit, the dog got tired. It
couldn't reach Tom, so turned and
went back to the house.
"Whew!" said Tom. "A lucky escape.
It should be safe to get down now."

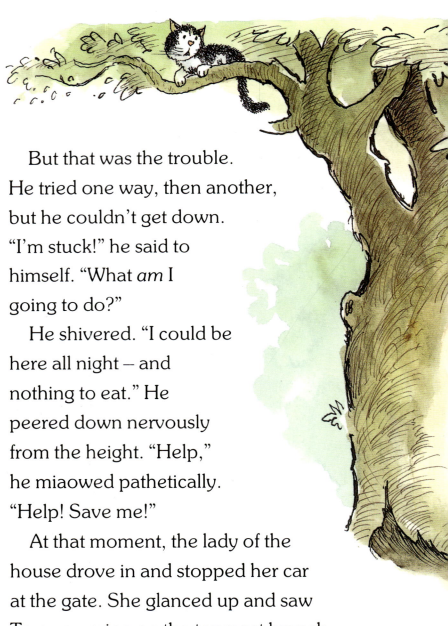

But that was the trouble.
He tried one way, then another,
but he couldn't get down.
"I'm stuck!" he said to
himself. "What *am* I
going to do?"

He shivered. "I could be
here all night – and
nothing to eat." He
peered down nervously
from the height. "Help,"
he miaowed pathetically.
"Help! Save me!"

At that moment, the lady of the
house drove in and stopped her car
at the gate. She glanced up and saw
Tom cowering on the topmost branch.
"Come down, puss, come down," she called.

"I can't," said poor Tom, and he clung on desperately.

"I know," said the lady. She went into the little house at the gate, and asked the lodgekeeper for help. He came out with a ladder, but he still couldn't reach Tom.

"Nothing for it," said the lady of the house briskly. "We'll have to call the fire brigade."

Tom was overcome with shame. "Oh, dear," he said. "I am in a mess, and it's all my own fault. I should never have made up that story to begin with."

The fire engine arrived with a clanging of bells. In no time at all, the fire-fighters had put up an extra long ladder and one of the fire-fighters climbed up and grabbed Tom.

By now a little crowd of people had gathered. They all cheered when the fire-fighter and Tom reached the ground safely.

"Is he one of ours?" asked the lady of the house.

"No, madam," said the lodgekeeper. "He's an outside cat."

The fire engine drove away and all the people went back to what they'd been doing. Tom slunk out of the gates. He was *so* ashamed.

"Hello, Tom." It was Smudge. "Fancy that!" he said. "I saw you stuck up that tree. Well, that was a tall story and no mistake."

Tom paid no attention, but made his way along the road, his tail and whiskers drooping sadly.

What was he going to do? He had to find a new job quickly. All the other cats would be laughing at him.

Chapter Three

Next day Tom was going past the village hall, feeling very low in spirits. Then he heard sounds from inside. There seemed to be quite a lot of noise and raised voices.

"I wonder what's happening in there," he said to himself and put his head round the door.

"We can't have actors that throw tantrums,"
said a grown-up voice. "It was a good idea, but
I think the cat will have to go."

"Who, me?" said Tom. He was
used to being in trouble by now.

But then he saw a small
girl carrying a large grey
fluffy cat who was struggling
in her arms.

As the girl and the cat
reached the way out,
the cat said, "That's it
then. I'm not going to
stay where I'm not wanted.
I've been in more
pantomimes than most
cats have had hot dinners.
And I was on a calendar
last Christmas but one.
I won't be bossed around."

"What happened?" asked Tom.

"Call it a bit of a dust-up," sniffed the cat. "I just don't like being bossed around. People banging tins and wanting you to run across the stage. No, thank you." He yawned. "So I told them. I hissed and spat."

The voice died away and the door swung to behind the girl and the grey cat.

But you could still hear the cat's voice. "I've been on a calendar. I told her."

Tom made his way towards the front of the
hall. On the stage a boy was sitting on a log.
He wore an old-fashioned costume and carried
a long stick with a red and white spotted
handkerchief tied to the end of it.

"Mrs Day," he said. "Here's another cat."

"Oh dear," said the lady in charge, "not
another."

"It's a bit scruffy-looking," said the boy.

"No more cats," said the lady firmly.

"But you can't have a Dick Whittington pantomime without a cat," said someone else.

Tom put on a face that said, "Look at me. I'm very clever and handsome and well-behaved."

"Anyone know where he comes from?" The lady in charge looked down at Tom.

"Looks like that cat that hangs around the butcher's," said someone.

"Well, all right," said the lady in charge. "If he's still around tomorrow night, he can be in the pantomime. Now let's get on with the rehearsal."

"A job!" thought Tom. "I'll turn up all right. I'll sleep in the hall and be as quiet as anything."

The job didn't seem to be very difficult. All he had to do was let the boy carry him on to the stage, then sit quietly while everyone else acted the play.

Later on, the lady said, "Let's see if he'll run across the stage. In the scene where he clears the palace of rats. Right? You hold him, Jamie, and someone bang the cat-food tin at the other side."

"Off you go, Puss." Jamie put Tom down on the stage, just as someone on the far side, out of sight, banged a tin with a spoon.

Tom ran from one side of the stage to the other. "Very good," said the lady. "Now if he can only do that tomorrow night."

Tom, cleaning the last morsel from the plate, raised his head and said, "You bet I can." But she didn't hear him.

A little later, when the rehearsal was over, he went outside. And there on the other side of the road, was Smudge.

"Hello," called Tom.

"Oh, it's you," said Smudge. "Still around? I thought you'd be off to the jungle or something like that."

"No time," said Tom. "I'm an actor in a pantomime."

"Nonsense." Smudge laughed. "I don't believe you."

"Please yourself," said Tom. "The village hall, tomorrow night. Better get there early. It's fully booked."

"Just another of his tall tales," thought Smudge.

But he thought he'd go along, just to see.

There was a large poster outside the hall.

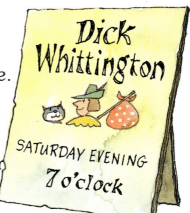

Dick Whittington

SATURDAY EVENING
7 o'clock

"I must find out what he's up to," said Smudge.

Next evening he crept into the hall and found a place on the window sill. He could hide behind the curtain and peep through the gap, to see what was happening.

Soon people began to arrive, and before long the hall was packed. Then there was a murmur of excitement and the curtains parted.

It was warm in the hall and Smudge became drowsy. He hardly followed the story of the pantomime – young Dick setting off to seek his fortune, and then arriving at the rich merchant's house.

He grew sleepier and sleepier so he hardly heard the cook scolding poor Dick. He never heard Dick in his miserable attic room, wishing he had never left home.

But all of a sudden Smudge woke up with a start. He peered through the curtains and he could hardly believe what he saw. There on the stage was Tom.

"Good puss," Dick was saying. "You will be my friend and help me – for I am all alone in the great city."

"Aw, isn't he lovely! Look at him." The audience could hardly take their eyes off Tom.

"It is – it really is him." Smudge was astonished.

At last, Tom, his tail held high, followed Dick off the stage. Everyone clapped and clapped.

Smudge was wide awake for the rest of the pantomime. Would Tom appear again?

38

The next act was set in the king's palace, in a strange country. And sure enough, Tom was carried on stage again.

"Who will rid the palace of these rats?" asked the king.

"I will." The ship's Captain stepped forward. "I have this wonderful animal, sent from England. Just see."

Tom raced across the stage. He was supposed to be chasing the rats away. The audience couldn't see the girl at the side of the stage. She was holding a saucer of cat food and banging a tin with a spoon. The audience cheered and cheered. Tom was the hit of the show.

At the end all the children in the pantomime took a bow. So did the lady who was in charge.

Someone presented her with a bunch of
flowers. Then the boy who played Dick
appeared. He carried Tom – and this time Tom
had a big red bow round his neck. All the
children cheered and stamped their feet. Tom
didn't mind the noise a bit. He knew they were
cheering him.

"Such a good cat. So well behaved." The
lady in charge patted Tom on the head.

A reporter from the local paper wrote all about Tom – "The Stray that Saved the Show". (That wasn't quite so, but certainly Tom had been a great success.)

"Where does he come from, I wonder?" said one of the actors.

"He's often around the butcher's shop," said another.

"But he doesn't belong there," said someone else. "He's a stray."

"Mrs Day," said the boy who had played Dick, "could I have him?"

"Well," the lady in charge paused. "You'd better ask your mum about that."

"I'd look after him properly," the boy promised. "Really I would."

"All right," Mum agreed. So they asked the butcher if they might take Tom home.

"'Course you can have him," said the butcher. "He doesn't belong anywhere."

Tom was delighted to have a real home at last. A cushion to sleep on, and meals once, twice, sometimes three times a day!

"So you really were an actor," said Smudge, next time Tom appeared.

"Of course." Tom yawned. "Didn't you believe me?"

"Tell us all about it." The other cats were longing to hear Tom's story.

So he sat down and told them what it was like, being on the stage. "Now," he said, "you must excuse me. I'm going home for a sleep. Acting is very tiring."

"Clever Tom," said a small tabby cat. "What will you do next?"

"I may not be around for a little time," said Tom airily. "My cousin Mooncat has asked me to stay."

"I've heard of the man in the moon," said Smudge, "but never the cat in the moon."

"No?" said Tom. "Then I'll tell you all about it when I get back."

Smudge and the other cats stared after him as he strolled off. It might be one of his tall tales. But with Tom, you could never be sure, could you?

They would watch out next full moon, just in case.

Look out for more exciting titles in the Storybooks series:

Judy and the Martian by Penelope Lively
Illustrated by Frank Rodgers

The Martian has only just passed his driving test, and is always losing his way. This time, he finds himself on planet Earth, hiding behind a freezer in a supermarket!

The King in the Forest by Michael Morpurgo
Illustrated by Tony Kerins

While a boy, Tod rescues a young fawn from the King's huntsmen. And many years later, Tod finds his loyalty to his old friend the deer put to the test . . .

The Midnight Moropus by Joan Aiken
Illustrated by Gavin Rowe

Jon knows of a strange story that, at midnight exactly, you can catch sight of a long-extinct horse at the waterfall. Jon becomes obsessed with the idea of catching a glimpse of the moropus . . .

Nigel The Pirate by Roy Apps
Illustrated by Scoular Andersen

Nigel's hopes of fun and adventure on the open seas are soon sunk on board *The Bloody Plunderer* . . .

Lizzie's War by Elisabeth Beresford
Illustrated by James Mayhew

When Lizzie's house is bombed during the war, she is sent to stay in the countryside with Miss Damps. How will Lizzie cope with her unfamiliar surroundings?

All these books can be purchased from your local bookseller. For more information about Storybooks, write to: *The Sales Department, Macdonald Young Books, 61 Western Road, Hove, East Sussex BN3 1JD.*

PRINTED IN BELGIUM BY
proost
INTERNATIONAL BOOK PRODUCTION

First published in Great Britain in 1994 by Simon & Schuster Young Books
Reprinted in 1996 by Macdonald Young Books

Typeset in 15/23pt Souvenir Light by Goodfellow & Egan Ltd, Cambridge

Macdonald Young Books
61 Western Road, Hove,
East Sussex BN3 1JD

British Library Cataloguing in Publication Data available

ISBN 0 7500 1451 2
ISBN 0 7500 1452 0 (pbk)

Class No. _____ J _____ Acc No. C87462

Author: FORSYTH, A. Loc: ~~7 APR 2000~~

0 9 AUG 2001

LEABHARLANN
CHONDAE AN CHABHAIN

1. **This book may be kept three weeks. It is to be returned on / before the last date stamped below.**
2. **A fine of 20p will be charged for every week or ...k a book is overdue.**

30 JUN 2000

0 4 AUG 2000

15 NOV 2000

2 7 DEC 2000

2 8 SEP 2001

29 FEB 2002

15 APR 2002

2 2 OCT 2003

Cavan withdrawn library